A ... Help From My FRIENDS

SCHOLASTIC INC.

New York Toronto London Auckland Sydney
Mexico City New Delhi Hong Kong Buenos Aires

ISBN-13: 978-0-439-02441-9
ISBN-10: 0-439-02441-2

Based on the TV series *Wow! Wow! Wubbzy!* as seen on Nick Jr.®, created by Bob Boyle.

12 11 10 9 8 7 6 5 4 3 2 1 7 8 9 10 11/0

Designed by Kim Brown

Printed in the U.S.A.
First printing, September 2007

"Can you help me eat all this cake?" asked Wubbzy.

"Yum!" they answered happily. "We'd love to!"

In fact, the whole town helped Wubbzy, Widget, and Walden eat the biggest chocolate doodleberry cake they had ever seen!

"Wow-wow-wow!" said Wubbzy.

Beep-Beep, Beep-Beep! Wubbzy was very excited! He had a new horn for his tooter-scooter.

Wubbzy asked his friend Widget if he could borrow a wiggle wrench so that he could put on the horn.

"No problemo," said Widget. "Let me help you." She took the scooter and put on the horn.

"But I didn't want anybody's help," Wubbzy said.

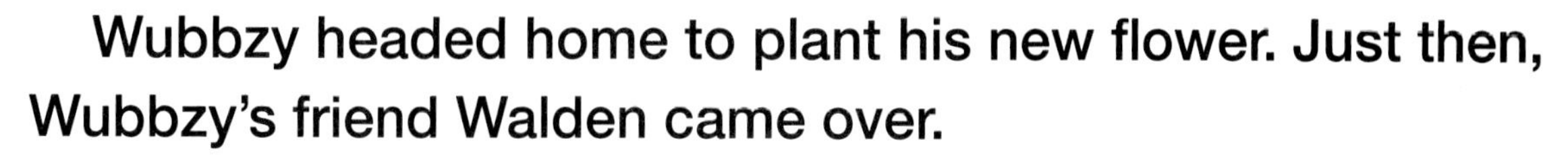

Wubbzy headed home to plant his new flower. Just then, Wubbzy's friend Walden came over.

"Hi, Wubbzy!" Walden said. "Be sure to fertilize that flower."

"But I don't know how," Wubbzy said.

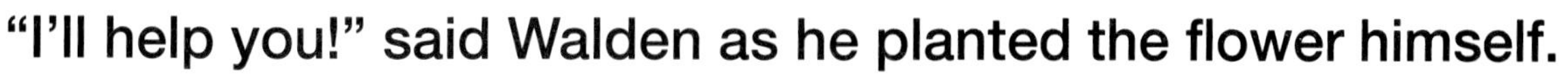

"I'll help you!" said Walden as he planted the flower himself.

Wubbzy was upset. He wanted to do things by himself. Then he had an idea.

"I'll make a chocolate doodleberry cake for Walden and Widget!" he said. "And I'll do it all by myself!"

Wubbzy added some super-duper baking powder to his cake. A whole lot of powder came out of the box!

"Oops!" he said. "Oh well, a little extra can't hurt!"

Before Wubbzy could put the cake in the oven, the batter started to grow . . . and grow . . . and grow!

"Yikes!" yelled Wubbzy. The cake was out of control! Soon, it was oozing out the door!

Walden and Widget were on their way to Wubbzy's house when they saw the huge wave of cake batter rush by. Wubbzy was riding on top!

"Help!" Wubbzy shouted.

"Oh, no!" yelled Walden. "The whole town is going to be covered in cake batter. We need to save Wubbzy! I'm going to need your help."

"No problemo," answered Widget.

"Wow-wow-wow!" called Wubbzy. "I'm heading right for the art museum! What am I going to do? I don't want to ruin the paintings!"

Walden pulled in front of the museum in a big truck. The cake batter hit the truck and turned away from the museum.

"Whew!" Walden sighed. "We saved the art museum just in time."

“Wow-wow-wow!” yelled Wubbzy. “I’m heading right for the zoo! Watch out, animals!”

"TIMBER!" shouted Walden. Just as the cake batter was about to hit the zoo, he chopped down a huge tree right in front of the entrance! The cake batter hit the tree and turned away from the zoo.

"Hooray!" said the zookeeper. "You saved all the animals!"

"Wow-wow-wow!" yelled Wubbzy. "I'm heading right for the library! What am I going to do? All of the books are going to be covered in batter!"

Walden quickly jumped into a crane and lowered a large pipe in front of the building. The cake batter (and Wubbzy!) went through the pipe, and turned away from the library.

"Whew!" said Walden. "Another save, just in the nick of time!"

All this time, Widget had been busy working on a new invention.

"Are you almost finished?" Walden called out.

"All done!" Widget replied. "Ta-da! It's the Big Bakey Oven 3000."

It was the BIGGEST oven the town had ever seen!

"Wow-wow-wow!" yelled Wubbzy. "This batter is heading straight for the oven. Somebody help me!"

Right before the cake rushed into the oven, Walden and his friend the giraffe scooped up Wubbzy just in time! The rest of the cake went into the oven and Widget closed the door.

"Wow," said Wubbzy. "What a mess! I really wanted to do something without anybody's help, but I guess it's not so bad to get some help from your friends now and then. Thanks!"

"No problemo," said Widget.

"Any time," said Walden.

"Hey, guys?" Wubbzy asked. "Could you help me out with something else?"